GRANPA

John Burningham

Also in Picture Puffins by John Burningham

MR GUMPY'S MOTOR CAR
MR GUMPY'S OUTING

Other Picture Puffins

ELEPHANT PIE *Hilda Offen*
THE SELFISH GIANT *Oscar Wilde & Michael Foreman/Freire Wright*
WAR AND PEAS *Michael Foreman*
PASS IT POLLY *Sarah Garland*
LUCY AND TOM AT THE SEASIDE *Shirley Hughes*

PUFFIN BOOKS

Published by the Penguin Group
Penguin Books Ltd, 27 Wrights Lane, London W8 5TZ, England
Penguin Putnam Inc., 375 Hudson Street, New York, New York 10014, USA
Penguin Books Australia Ltd, Ringwood, Victoria, Australia
Penguin Books Canada Ltd, 10 Alcorn Avenue, Toronto, Ontario, Canada M4V 3B2
Penguin Books (NZ) Ltd, Private Bag 102902, NSMC, Auckland, New Zealand

Penguin Books Ltd, Registered Offices: Harmondsworth, Middlesex, England

First published by Jonathan Cape Ltd 1984
Published in Picture Puffins 1988
16 18 20 19 17

Copyright © John Burningham, 1984
All rights reserved

Made and printed in Italy by Printers Trento Srl

And how's my little girl?

There would not be room for all the little seeds to grow.

Do worms go to Heaven?

One man went to mow
Went to mow a meadow...

*Little ducks, soup and sheep, sunshine in
the trees...*

I didn't know Teddy was another
little girl.

Noah knew that the ark was not far from land when he saw the dove carrying the olive branch.

Could we float away in this house, Granpa?

That was not a nice thing

to say to Granpa.

This is a lovely chocolate ice-cream.

It's not chocolate, it's strawberry.

When we get to the beach can we stay there for ever?

Yes, but we must go back for our tea at four o'clock.

When I've finished this lolly can we get some more? I need the sticks to make things.

When I was a boy we used to roll our
wooden hoops down the street
after school.

Were you once a baby as well, Granpa?

If I catch a fish we can cook it for supper.

What if you catch a whale, Granpa?

Harry, Florence and I used to come
down that hill like little arrows.
I remember one Christmas…

You nearly slipped then, Granpa.

Granpa can't come out to play today.

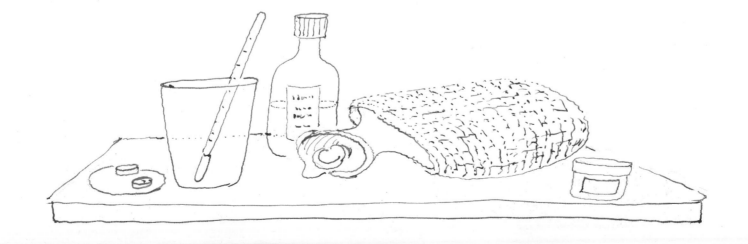

Tomorrow shall we go to Africa, and you can be the captain?